LUCY

For Barbara McClatchey and everyone else at Second Chance Poms,

who rescued the real Lucy and gave her to me

◆ ◆ ◆

First edition 2016

Library of Congress Catalog Card Number 2015934395
ISBN 978-0-7636-6808-2

16 17 18 19 20 21 CCP 10 9 8 7 6 5 4 3 2 1

Printed in Shenzhen, Guangdong, China

This book was typeset in Filosofia.
The illustrations were done in oil.

Candlewick Press
99 Dover Street
Somerville, Massachusetts 02144

visit us at www.candlewick.com

LUCY

RANDY CECIL

CANDLEWICK PRESS

ACT I

· 1 ·

As the sun rose over Bloomville,
a distant trumpet began to play—
doodle-de-doodle-doo.

The notes drifted through the streets, past the shops,
down the alley where the little dog slept,
and into her dreams.

And then a car door slammed.

She was awake now.

And she was off!

Past Bertolt's Butcher Shop . . .

Past the diner with the questionable scraps . . .

No time for the one-eyed cat in the window

or the silly pigeons in the park . . .

Around the corner with the fire hydrant and across the street . . .

Down the block and up the steps
of the apartment building with the red door . . .

She sat.

· 2 ·

Inside the apartment building with the red door,
Eleanor Wische opened an old steamer trunk. She pushed
aside the baseball glove, the box of chalk, and her father's
snow-globe collection and took out a ball of string.

She hugged her father good-bye as he rushed to get ready for work,
and took the ball of string into her room.

Tying the end of the string around a bit of sausage
she had sneaked from breakfast, she leaned out her window.

She unwound the string, and down went the sausage,
lower and lower . . .

to the little dog waiting below.

3

As he was leaving for work, Sam Wische noticed that the old steamer trunk had been left open. He went to close it when, next to the baseball glove and the box of chalk, he saw his snow-globe collection.

He took out the Paris globe and watched as snow swirled around the tiny Eiffel Tower. Then, taking all the snow globes into his arms, he threw Paris into the air.

Next he threw the London globe and then Tokyo, Istanbul,
and Cairo—all the places he dreamed of someday seeing.
They circled around him in perfect order.
He was juggling.

He sat on the edge of the dining-room table and closed his eyes —
and he was still juggling.

He lay down — and he was still juggling.

He moved from room to room, eyes closed, while the snow globes
circled through the air in perfect order.

Suddenly he heard the cuckoo clock. He was late for work.
He packed the snow globes in his juggling case,
grabbed his keys, stepped outside . . .

and nearly tripped over the little dog
sitting at his door.

4

After breakfast, the little dog roamed the streets of Bloomville.
She chased the pigeons in the park. She barked at the one-eyed cat.

And when the sun was high in the sky and the concrete sidewalks grew hot,
she retreated to the shady doorway of Harry's Barbershop for a nap.

There, in her dreams, she remembered her former life . . .

She is on the hunt, prowling down long halls
and into quiet bedrooms.

She searches balconies and verandas,
and behind curtains and cabinets and vases.

She lies in wait under the dining-room table.

And she surveys the unused study from atop the tallest chair.

Finally, in defeat, she climbs up on a soft couch.
And there, hiding behind the cushion, her elusive prey . . .

Her stuffed toy cat!

· 5 ·

Sam had arrived late for work, and his boss was not pleased.
So he quickly unpacked crates and he carefully stocked shelves,
and he did not juggle . . .

until his boss stepped outside.

· 6 ·

Eleanor placed a quarter on the counter at Enzo's Deli.
And Enzo handed her a cheese sandwich and her change, a nickel.

Eleanor took her lunch and dropped the nickel into her pocket
along with all the other nickels from previous lunches.

On her way home she saw Dahlia and Daisy
on their afternoon walk with Mrs. del Rio.

And she said hello to Bailey and Mrs. Pennington.

She blew a kiss to Henry, the Labrador who kept watch over
the neighborhood from his third-floor apartment.

Eleanor thought about what she would call
the little dog she gave breakfast to, if the little dog were hers.
Probably Lucy, she thought. *Yes, Lucy.*

And where is Lucy now? she wondered.

As evening approached, Lucy positioned herself
across the street from Bertolt's Butcher Shop.

Mrs. Pennington ambled by
on her last walk of the day with Bailey.

And Mrs. del Rio strolled leisurely past
with Dahlia and Daisy.

Lucy sniffed a mailbox.

She pretended to inspect a lamppost.

Then she crossed the quiet street.
And when the moment was right, Lucy made her move . . .

In through the door of Bertolt's Butcher Shop
and out again in a flash . . .

her prize bouncing along behind her.

· 8 ·

By the time Sam arrived at the Palace Theater, the Amazing Konn
was already onstage. He performed the usual card tricks and
pulled a rabbit from a hat, and the audience responded
with a polite smattering of applause.

But they gasped as he sawed his lovely assistant in half.
And they burst into thunderous applause when her lower half
jumped up and danced across the stage.

The Amazing Konn took a bow and the curtain swung closed.
Then it was Sam's turn.

He took the snow globes from his juggling case
as the curtain swung open again.

He threw the Paris snow globe into the air, and then London, Tokyo,
Istanbul, and Cairo. The globes circled around him in perfect order.
And then he looked out into the audience . . .

Suddenly he was petrified. He felt dizzy, and his hands went numb.
The Paris globe fell to the stage floor with a crack.
And then London, Tokyo, Istanbul, and Cairo, one at a time,
shattered all around him.

The audience fell silent as a large hook reached out
and pulled Sam from the stage.

As he left the theater, he turned to see
Umberto the Boneless Wonder tying himself into a knot.
The audience applauded politely.

And the curtain swung closed.

ACT II

· 1 ·

The next morning, as the sun rose over Bloomville,
a distant trumpet once again began to play —
doodle-de-doodle-doo —
followed by a trombone — *womp-wah, womp-wah.*

The notes lifted into the air and mingled among the treetops in the park,
then fell to the streets, drifting down the alley where Lucy slept
and into her dreams.

And then a car horn honked.

She was awake now.

And she was off!

Past Bertolt the angry butcher . . .

Past the diner with the questionable scraps . . .

No time for the one-eyed cat in the window

or the silly pigeons in the park . . .

Around the corner with the fire hydrant and across the street . . .

Down the block and up the steps
of the apartment building with the red door . . .

She sat.

Inside the apartment building with the red door, Eleanor opened the old steamer trunk. She pushed aside the baseball glove and the box of chalk, took out the ball of string, and closed the trunk.

She hugged her father good-bye as he got ready for work.
Then she took the ball of string into her room.

She tied the string around a bit of cheese
saved from yesterday's lunch and leaned out her window.

She unwound the string. Down went the bit of cheese,
lower and lower . . .

to the little dog waiting below.

And as she rolled the string back up,
Eleanor smiled and waved to Dahlia and Daisy,
out on their morning walk with Mrs. del Rio.

· 3 ·

Back inside the apartment, Sam cleared the dishes from the table.
But he did not juggle them.
Instead, he packed them in his juggling case.

He stepped outside and scooted around
the little dog at his door.

He saw Mrs. del Rio approaching with something on her mind.

Was she saying something about a window? And string?

Sam did not wait around to find out.

He would not be late today.

After breakfast, Lucy once again roamed the streets of Bloomville.
She passed the homes of other dogs. Most were back inside now,
napping on soft couches or chewing on treats.

And when the sun was high in the sky and the concrete grew hot,
she moved to the cool green grass of the park,
where she curled up next to a shady bush for a nap.

There, in her dreams, Lucy remembered her former life . . .

She is outside on a porch, lying upon a velvet tufted bench.
She is guarding her stuffed toy cat.

A suspicious-looking bird flutters and hops, closer and closer.
Lucy barks, and the bird flies away.

She hears the jingle of a collar and rushes to
find an unfamiliar dog snooping around the back gate.
She barks, and it runs away.

She sees two sneaky squirrels creeping through the grass.
She charges across the lawn, and they scamper
up a tree and disappear over a wall.

Finally, with her rivals in retreat,
Lucy returns to the porch, to her prize.

Her stuffed toy cat.

· 5 ·

For days, Sam Wische had been carefully constructing a display
in front of the store—a tower of canned soup.

As he started on a row of minestrone,
he noticed the street was quiet and empty.

He threw a can into the air.
And then he threw another and another, until canned soup
was circling around him in perfect order.

And then the McGinty family stepped around the corner.
Sam felt dizzy and his hands went numb.

· 6 ·

A dog should have toys, thought Eleanor.
So she selected an armful of stuffed toys from a basket and
placed them on the counter of Mrs. Chi's Pet Shop.
And as she counted out her leftover lunch-money nickels,
Mrs. Chi placed the toys in a brown paper bag.

On her way home she saw the McGinty family in the park.

She smiled as she watched Emily McGinty playing fetch with Scooter.

And she laughed as she watched little Billy chase Rex around a tree.

Or was Rex chasing Billy?

All the while, she thought about Lucy.

And she wondered where Lucy was now.

Back on the street, she passed the store where her father worked.

Canned soup was everywhere.

· 7 ·

In the afternoon, as Lucy once again grew hungry,
she passed by Bertolt's Butcher Shop.

But Bertolt was guarding the door more closely than ever.

She came across a few cans of soup on the street,
but the cans were unopened.

Everywhere she looked there was food.
But none of it was for her.

And so she found herself in the alley behind the diner,
sniffing some leftover scraps of food.
These were questionable scraps. Very questionable.

She ate them anyway.

· 8 ·

Sam arrived at the Palace Theater just as the curtain opened on
the Dixie Sisters. They played banjos and sang in three-part harmony,
and the audience applauded politely.

During their next number, they circled gracefully around the stage.
As they sped up and moved into a figure eight, their dresses
lifted just enough to reveal they were riding on unicycles.

The crowd burst into thunderous applause.

The curtain closed, and Sam stepped onto the stage.
He opened his juggling case and took out the dishes.

The curtain opened again. Taking a deep breath, Sam tossed a cup
into the air. Next he tossed a bowl, followed by a glass, then another cup
and another bowl. The dishes circled around him in perfect order.
And then he looked out into the audience . . .

Suddenly he was petrified. He felt dizzy, and his hands went numb.
The first glass fell to the stage and shattered.
And then a bowl shattered, followed by a cup,
then the other cup and the other bowl.

The audience fell silent as, once again,
the large hook reached out and pulled Sam from the stage.

As he left the theater, he turned to see one of
Mr. B.'s fantastic fleas walking across a tightrope.
The audience applauded politely.

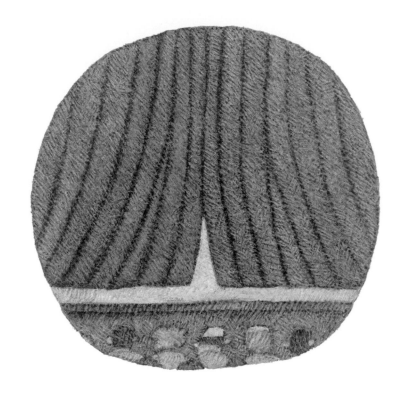

And the curtain swung closed.

ACT III

· 1 ·

The next morning, as the sun rose over Bloomville,
a distant trumpet once again began to play—*doodle-de-doodle-doo*—
followed by a trombone—*womp-wah, womp-wah*—
and finally a double bass—*bompa-bomp, bompa-bomp.*

The notes rose upward and joined together as beautiful music,
among the rooftops and water towers, then fell gently to the streets,
down the alley where Lucy slept, and into her dreams.

And then a car backfired.

She was awake now.

And she was off!

Past Bertolt's Butcher Shop . . .

Past the diner with the questionable scraps . . .

No time for the one-eyed cat in the window

or the silly pigeons in the park . . .

Around the corner with the fire hydrant and across the street . . .

Down the block and up the steps
of the apartment building with the red door . . .

She sat.

Eleanor had noticed that her father's snow-globe collection was missing.
And she was aware, too, of their ever-shrinking set of dishes.
Her father needed to practice. He needed to practice in front of an audience.

So now, instead of giving the bit of sausage in her pocket
(not to mention a new stuffed toy) to the little dog waiting downstairs,
she was sitting patiently on the couch—
an audience of one.

She attempted an encouraging smile as her father returned from
the kitchen with their few remaining dishes and began throwing them
into the air. Around and around the dishes went,
flying through the air in perfect order.

And then, one at a time, the dishes came to rest in his hand.

Eleanor applauded, and Sam took a bow.

· 3 ·

Feeling emboldened, Sam Wische packed the dishes in his
juggling case. And then he took some fruit from the kitchen
and a brown paper bag filled with stuffed toys
and packed it all in his juggling case.

He said good-bye to his daughter, and, being careful not to trip
over the little dog at his door, he stepped outside.

But the little dog was not there.

· 4 ·

And where was Lucy? She was roaming the streets of Bloomville,
following anyone who looked like they might drop a doughnut or
let a bit of strudel slip through their fingers. But no one did.

So, when the sun was high in the sky and the sidewalks grew hot,
she once again returned to the cool green park,
where she curled up under a shady tree for a nap.

There, in her dreams, Lucy remembered her former life . . .

She is on a picnic in a park, far away from home.
And she is on the prowl again, searching for her stuffed toy cat.
She searches inside the picnic basket and beneath the blanket.

She searches in some nearby bushes and behind an old oak tree.
But her elusive prey is nowhere to be found.

Then she sees some pigeons pecking at the ground near the edge of the park.
She charges toward them, and they fly away,
landing again a block up the street.

She charges again, and again they fly away.
And it is here that Lucy sees a most unusual sight . . .

There, sitting in a window across the street, is a one-eyed cat.
She crosses the street and barks at the cat, but it doesn't move.
So she barks some more.
And then a strange scent wafts by.

Entranced, Lucy follows the peculiar smell down the street
and around a corner or two (or is it three?).
On and on she walks, paying little attention to the shops,
people, and dogs along the way.

She slips through a hole in a fence, and there, in an alley behind a diner,
is the source of the unusual odor — leftover scraps of food.
She takes a big sniff. These are questionable scraps. Very questionable.
She eats them anyway.

With a full belly, she slips back through the hole in the fence.
The street is quiet and night is falling.
And only then does she realize she is lost.
Completely and utterly lost.

While Lucy slept, Sam was out in the street opening his juggling case.
He took out five pieces of fruit and started to juggle.
Soon after, Mrs. del Rio approached from one direction
and Mrs. Pennington approached from another.

And just like that, Sam Wische was juggling in front of an audience —
an audience of two!

Sam packed the fruit back in his juggling case
and ran down the street.

He stopped near a stoop where a boy was sitting, and he started
to juggle again. A moment later, Mrs. del Rio and Mrs. Pennington
caught back up to him. And just like that, Sam Wische was juggling
in front of an audience — an audience of three!

Again Sam rushed down the street, and the small crowd followed.

He stopped in front of Enzo's Deli and began juggling again.

Fruit was flying through the air when a customer stepped out the door.

An audience of four!

Finally Enzo poked his head out the door
of his deli to see what was going on —
an audience of five!

· 6 ·

By the time Eleanor made it to her bedroom window,
Lucy was gone. So, with the bit of sausage from breakfast
still in her pocket, she set out to find her.

She asked Enzo at the deli if he had seen the little white dog.
He had not.

She asked Bertolt at the butcher shop if he had seen the little white dog.
He had not.

She searched everywhere, from busy streets to empty back alleys.
But Lucy was nowhere to be found.

The sun was setting as she entered the park.
A large crowd of people was laughing and clapping.

Eleanor pushed her way through the crowd to find
her father packing his juggling case.
She asked if he had seen the little white dog.
He had not.

· 7 ·

From deep within Eleanor's pocket, the faintest scent of sausage
rose into the air. It drifted over a park bench, around a tree,
and past Lucy's nose.

She awakened with a jolt to see the girl who fed her breakfast
and her father. They were walking away.

She followed them through the darkening streets.

She lost them for a moment in a crowd gathered under a marquee,
but picked up the scent again just in time to see them enter
the back door of a theater.

She waited and watched, and finally the door opened again.

A man on stilts stepped out, and Lucy made her move . . .

She dashed between the extra-long legs and into the theater in a flash!

Backstage, the Palace Theater was bustling with people and activities of every sort, but the girl and her father were nowhere in sight.

Yet the scent of sausage remained.

Lucy pushed through a maze of velvet curtains and suddenly
found herself at the edge of a stage.
She did not see the girl anywhere, but she did see the girl's father.
He was standing on the stage, throwing fruit into the air.

· 8 ·

Oranges, apples, and pears flew through the air in perfect order
and finally came to rest in Sam's hand one piece at a time.
He took a bow.

And there was a polite smattering of applause from the audience.

Sam turned to his juggling case in search of something better,
more exciting, than fruit. He settled on the stuffed toys.
He turned back to the audience, took a deep breath, and threw
a stuffed toy bird into the air. Then he threw another bird,
followed by a stuffed squirrel, and then another stuffed squirrel.
And finally he threw a stuffed toy cat into the air.

Suddenly, out of the corner of his eye,
he saw a little dog charging toward him.

It leaped through the air.
In an instant Sam was down on the ground.

But he was still juggling!

The little dog jumped onto his chest and then
up to his flailing shins, leaping from one leg to another,
snapping and barking at the toys circling above.

But he was still juggling!

Finally, the little dog snatched the toy cat out of the air.
Sam, having now completely lost his bearings, watched as one by one
the rest of the toys fell to the ground with soft thuds.

Sam Wische lay on the stage expecting to hear the audience booing.
He expected the hook to reach out and pull him from the stage. But it didn't.
Instead he heard applause — wild, thunderous applause.

And the curtain swung closed.

ACT IV

The next morning, Eleanor watched as her father juggled
a brand-new set of dishes. There was no rush.
Lucy was not outside on the stoop waiting for her breakfast.
Lucy was here, right next to Eleanor.

As the dishes came to rest, one at a time, in Sam's hand, Eleanor applauded.
Sam took a bow, and Lucy stretched and yawned and curled up for a nap.

And in her dreams Lucy saw her new life . . .

just exactly as it was.